When You Were *Not Jenny*

When You Were *Not Jenny* Again

Ann Bernath

ReadAnnBernath Publishing
Duarte, CA | readannbernath.com

ISBN: 9798342035804

Printed by Kindle Direct Publishing in the United States of America

When You Were
Not Jenny

Ann Bernath

J enny Coulter was the last person Matt
expected to see standing on his front stoop.
He barely knew her. Even after two years
working in the same department, they had only
exchanged a handful of short sentences. In
fact, he couldn't think of anyone from work
who had visited him at home or even knew
where he lived. He and his colleagues
socialized at bars or restaurants, and he
couldn't remember Jenny ever attending. Yet,
there she stood, in her long brown raincoat
and matching umbrella, waiting for him to
answer his doorbell.

He backed away from the peephole,
unlocked the deadbolt, and pulled the door

1

open.

"Jenny?"

She looked up at him from under the hood of her raincoat, wisps of her dark hair escaping her short ponytail, some teasing at, others clinging to, her rosy cheeks.

"Hello, Matt," she said. "How are you?"

Her voice, friendly and light, matched her smile, but her large, glistening eyes suggested a sadder story.

"I'm fine." He flashed her a small, and no doubt quizzical, smile. "What brings you out on this rainy night?"

She lifted the cup she was holding in her free hand, positioned it so he could see *The Perfect Grind* logo printed on its side.

"Cappuccino," she said.

He nodded. He, too, often braved the elements for a caffeine fix. Of course, this didn't explain why she was at his doorstep.

He opened the door a little wider. "Did you want to come in?"

Jenny took a small step backward, started to shake her head.

"Just for a minute?" He opened the door

wider. "Come on in and warm up."

She studied his face for a long, uncomfortable moment before she nodded.

"All right. Just for a minute."

She stepped inside and Matt closed the door behind her, pointed to the umbrella stand and coat tree in the entryway.

"Umbrella? Raincoat?"

Slowly, almost reluctantly, she slipped out of her raincoat and hung it on the coat tree, then placed her umbrella in the umbrella stand.

"I can't stay long," she said.

He nodded. "Come on in and have a seat."

Matt led her into the living room and gestured toward the couch. As she sat, he lowered himself onto the edge of his recliner across from her.

She scanned the room, her hands in her lap, surveying his bookshelves and extensive vinyl record collection.

Somehow, she seemed different. Matt had sensed a difference immediately when he had seen her standing on his stoop. He knew seeing someone "out of context" could be a little jarring – street clothes instead of work clothes, a casual persona instead of a professional one. He had experienced that situation many times. But studying her now, he hardly recognized her stiff posture. He couldn't shake the feeling that whatever he had noticed about Jenny in the periphery of his awareness had changed, most notably, the way she looked at him, like now, when she turned once again to study his face.

Matt put his hands on his thighs and tried a slight smile, but he was starting to feel uneasy. He didn't like awkward silences, and this was fast becoming one.

"So," he said. "What brings you here?"

She lifted her eyebrows, as if he had caught her off-guard. "Oh. Yes. Presentation materials for the quarterlies are due tomorrow."

He waited for her to say more. When she didn't, he shifted into a different, and hopefully more comfortable, position.

"O – kay. Noted. But, is that why you're here? Are you sure you didn't have anything else to tell me?"

He noticed that she didn't look like she had

dressed to go visiting on a cold, rainy night. Her baggy sweatpants and sweatshirt seemed more like loungewear for watching TV, or in a pinch, running out for a cappuccino.

Her gaze softened, the happy-but-sad look in her eyes returning.

"No, that's all." She rose. "I'll get going now."

"Well, here, let me heat that up for you at least before you go."

He reached for her cup at the same time she was turning, and their hands collided, splashing the hot liquid out through the hole in the lid and onto her hand.

She gasped.

"I'm so sorry! I'll get a towel."

He ran to the kitchen, pulled a towel from the refrigerator handle, then raced back into the living room.

"Here --"

"Matt James?!"

Jenny stood staring at him, her eyebrows lifting high onto her forehead, her free hand reaching for her throat, her other, still-dripping hand, holding her cup out in front of her.

"Where am I? What's going on?"

"You . . . I spilled your drink on you," Matt said.

He reached out with the towel, but she recoiled away from him, her gaze darting wildly around the room.

"Where am I?" She started breathing harder.

"It's okay, Jenny."

He almost told her to calm down, but remembered he never reacted well to people who told him to calm down. On the other hand, he didn't know what else to do. She seemed to be panicking.

She suddenly dropped back down onto the couch.

Matt started to panic a bit himself. What had just happened?

Setting the towel on the coffee table, he sat slowly back down across from her, watched as she closed her eyes, drew in a gasping breath followed by several calmer ones, waited until her eyes finally fluttered open again.

She grabbed the towel, wiped her hand and

the cup, and then put the towel back onto the table.

"I knew this was a mistake," she said. He didn't think the statement was meant for him. She drew in a deep breath and met his gaze. "I shouldn't have done this. I'm sorry, Matt. I'm going to go now."

She started to stand up. He threw his arm out, motioned her back down.

"No, don't rush off. What's going on? What happened just now?" He couldn't let her leave after . . . whatever that had been. "Something's wrong, isn't it? Do you need my help? Is that why you really stopped by? You need help, right?"

She shook her head. "No need to worry. I'm fine now."

Again, she tried to stand and he waved her back down.

Matt wished he had paid more attention during the company's mandatory mental health awareness training.

"Listen, Jenny. Tomorrow, I'll go with you to HR, to Employee Services. I'm sure they can get you some help."

Her eyes widened. "No, don't do that."

"It's no trouble."

"Please don't. Matt, please don't do anything. Please forget I stopped by. It was a big mistake." She set her cup down on the coffee table so she could rub her face with both hands. "A huge mistake."

He reached his hands out toward her. "Don't worry. You don't have to go. I can go to employee services for you and let them know and – "

"Matt!"

He sat back, stared at her frightened eyes. What was he to do? He seemed to just be upsetting her now.

She swallowed, shook her head.

"I can't believe I've done this. On a whim, a selfish whim," she said.

She sighed a deep, heavy sigh, reached back and removed her shoulder-length hair from the scrunchy restraining it, shook it free. Then she fixed her gaze on his. The Jenny Coulter he sort-of-knew had barely made eye contact before, let alone stared at him so intensely that he felt like his soul was exposed.

"I can't have you thinking Jenny is mentally ill and trying to get her help or in any other way interfering," she said.

His chest tightened. Had she just referred to herself in the third person?

"Matt, I'm going to tell you something now and you aren't going to believe me, at all, but please listen until I'm finished. Then, maybe I can think of some way to prove it to you."

She dropped her head briefly, then drew in another audible breath before looking up again to meet his gaze.

He waited, his mind reeling. He felt the long moment pass as if he were watching the secondhand crawl slowly around the clock face.

"I'm not who you think I am."

He felt his eyebrows go up, opened his mouth, remembered her admonition, clamped it shut again.

Identity crisis. Was that what this was? Or maybe a split personality?

"This is Jenny Coulter," she continued, gesturing to herself, "but you aren't talking to her now. I am someone else, someone who is temporarily inhabiting Jenny's mind."

He had forced his eyebrows down, but they shot up again.

Jenny drew in another breath. "Like I said, I know you won't believe me until I can prove it to you, but please, first, just listen."

Her voice, tentative at first, steadied. She seemed to truly believe what she was saying. Her dark eyes looked clear and lucid, not to mention a lovely shade of milk chocolate.

"Tomorrow, Jenny will experience an incident that will leave her in such a traumatized state that she won't recall, or can't bring herself to recount, what happened. Because she's in that state of mind, I'm able to occupy her consciousness in her own past, to witness the event so her therapists and I can help her."

Matt stared, fully aware his mouth had dropped slightly agape. Jenny's delusion seemed surprisingly detailed and beyond credulity. Not only did she think she was someone else who had possessed Jenny, she thought she was someone from the future.

"I am one of a handful that possess this ability. We're called Temporal Empathic Sensors. I can take a backseat, if you will, in a person's mind. I can also, for very brief periods, take control of a consciousness." She turned away to look out Matt's front windows, then turned back. "Until today, I had never actually tried it - taking control, I mean. But your house is between the coffee shop and Jenny's apartment, and when she glanced across the street, and I saw your lights were on . . ."

She shook her head.

Matt nodded, slowly, as if everything she had just said had made sense to him. He had to admit that, from her obviously deluded perspective, it made some kind of sense.

As subtly as he could, he leaned back in his chair, ran the fingers of both hands through his hair, gripped the strands and pulled, gently at first, then harder, to keep himself from reacting in some way that would upset her.

"I need you to do something for me, Matt," she said.

He dropped his hands back onto his thighs, gripped them, forced a smile.

He didn't know how to react at this point. She had woven him into her fantasy, even if she had claimed that she didn't expect him to believe her.

"I need you to forget I came here and told you any of this." Her tone was commanding.

"Please just return to your normal routine. Don't interfere. Let me help Jenny."

He didn't answer. His expression, though, must have communicated that he couldn't possibly forget what he had just seen, that he clearly meant to go to employee services first thing in the morning, for she sighed a deep, long, resigned sigh.

"All right. I need to prove it to you, don't I?"

He shook his head slowly from side to side, gave a small shrug of his shoulders.

"I'm sorry, Jenny, but I don't think you can."

Jenny bit her lip, moved to the very edge of her chair and leaned as far forward as she could.

"I didn't come prepared, obviously." She closed her eyes, shook her head, as if she were silently scolding herself. She opened her eyes again. "If I had known I would be in this predicament, I would have looked up the scores for tomorrow's basketball or football or tennis results – whichever season is happening now – or told you about some worldwide event. Instead, I'll need to try something else."

She waited until he was paying attention, for he was still planning how he might explain everything to employee services the next morning, and his gaze had drifted to the floor. But her silence caught his attention, and he raised his eyes to meet that unnerving, penetrating gaze.

"Okay."

He felt he needed to say something.

"Tonight," she said, "when you write in your journal, add a phrase or reference or quote that you know you've never mentioned to anyone. Tomorrow morning, I'll meet you at *The Perfect Grind* on your way to work and I'll tell you what you wrote."

So far, he had been successful keeping his mind from attempting to solve a logic puzzle that couldn't be solved, but he couldn't let this go unquestioned.

"How do you know about my journal?" His kinder, cautious tone had disappeared. "Do you plan to break in? Have you bugged my apartment? Are you using some kind of spy camera?"

"No! No, nothing like that. This is what I'm trying to explain, Matt. If you're afraid I can sneak in, lock your journal up." She sighed again. "It won't make any difference."

She looked directly into his eyes with that same look --happy to see him, sad to see him. It matched the bittersweet tone of her voice.

"Where I am, in your future," she said, and she paused for a beat, "I have access to your journal."

A silent second passed. He felt a small chill radiate from his neck down into his shoulders. She really knew how to spin a story.

"Please, Matt. Give me a chance to prove it to you before you do something rash."

She needed help. He felt certain. But, maybe indulging her request would help her to realize that she really didn't know what he had written, and perhaps then, over coffee, he could convince her to get that help.

He nodded to her. "All right. I'll think of something," he said.

She smiled in relief. "Thank you. I have to go now. I can't keep control for much longer, and you saw what happens when I lose control." She stood. "I need to get Jenny back home. Hopefully, she'll believe she had a strange dream."

She moved to the door, slipped into her raincoat, and grabbed the umbrella. Matt jumped up from his seat to follow her.

Should he let her leave? What else should he say to her? She opened the door, pushed the hood back up over her head, and turned back to look at him.

"Remember, some kind of reference or phrase. Choose something that you feel absolutely certain no one could possibly guess. Add it to your journal with today's date. I'll meet you for coffee at your usual time." She gave him that smile, that look that he couldn't remember having seen on Jenny Coulter before. "Goodnight, Matt."

He followed her to the doorway and watched her disappear into the misty dusk.

When he stepped back inside, he stood for a moment staring at the place where Jenny had been standing, her eyes wide and frightened, suddenly unaware of her whereabouts. He could do this small thing for her.

He moved to his bedroom, pulled his journal from his nightstand, and ran his fingers over the old, smooth leather. He loved this journal. His grandfather had given it to him, and he felt close to him whenever he cracked the binding and spread it flat across his desk. He had seen pictures of his grandfather as a young man and the resemblance was a keen one. Tall, hazel eyes, reddish-blond hair that was too straight and fine to lie flat without product, and a wink of mischief, his mother said. His grandfather had always kept a short beard, though, while Matt preferred a well-groomed scruff.

At first, Matt had journaled faithfully, describing people he'd seen on his walk to work as if they were characters in his own life story, imagining what had brought them to that moment, detailing unique characteristics and selecting those who would make good protagonists. He'd written short vignettes inspired by the people he'd observed, the books he'd read, and the music he'd listened to, and then he'd read those entries aloud to his grandfather when he'd visited him at the nursing home. His grandfather had smiled and chuckled, and Matt had looked forward to every visit. But after his grandfather had passed away, Matt had stopped writing. No journaling of daily events or musings. No vignettes or character sketches. Nothing real or imagined had seemed important or worthy enough to memorialize in the pages of that beautiful journal, so now the leather-bound book stayed in his nightstand untouched.

Matt straightened his shoulders, sat down at his desk.

Where was his pen? He rifled through the drawer and came up with one, even though it wasn't his favorite. It had a darker blue ink than he liked. But it wouldn't matter for this insane exercise. He opened the journal to the next blank page and wrote the date.

He sat for a long moment, staring at the blank lines. He spun his mental rolodex of favorite movies, TV shows, books, discounting them one by one as too popular, too well known, too obvious. He thought of older movies and books, turned to science fiction to be more obscure perhaps, and finally decided on a quote. The quote came from a series of books called The Lensmen that he knew he had never discussed with anyone since he'd read them when he was twelve. "Clear ether!" was his favorite quote. If the "ether" was clear, conditions were favorable and ships could launch. Characters also used it to wish each other farewell. The quote should suffice.

Just as he was about to write, he wondered if Jenny really had found some way to watch him. If she had, she would be able to tell him the quote, think that she had proved her story to him, and nothing would be resolved.

He stood, took the journal and pen with him to the front room, then slipped on his raincoat and stepped outside into the cold. Luckily, the rain had stopped for now. He walked down the street and around the corner to a bus stop and took a seat on the bench. Using the light from the canopy, he turned his journal to the new page and wrote, "'Clear ether!' -- E. E. 'Doc' Smith." He glanced over what he had written and decided the probability that someone could guess it was extremely small.

An inner voice popped up to cross-examine his convictions. What if she did tell him the quote? Would it just be an incredibly lucky guess?

The more unsettling question was, would he believe her?

He shook his head. What was he thinking? Of course not. He liked fantasy and sci-fi fiction, but he had never given any credence to ghost stories or supernatural tales or time travel speculation.

"I have access to your journal," she had said.

He swallowed.

For reasons he desperately wanted to attribute to the cold, Matt shuddered.

Matt James arrived at *The Perfect Grind* at the same time every weekday morning, so consistently that someone could set their watch by his arrival. But today, he had raced here and arrived a few minutes early, only to stop just outside the doors to look up at the threatening gray clouds overhead. Which of Jenny's personalities would be waiting for him inside? The one with frightened eyes who might not remember their conversation at all, or the one concocting a delusional tale of science fiction?

"After you."

He turned. Someone was holding the door open for him.

The version of Jenny who met his gaze with intense anticipation motioned him over to her table.

He slipped through the line of people waiting to order and took a seat across from her, perched himself on the edge of the seat. His knee started to bounce up and down.

She didn't speak for a moment. Finally, she drew in a breath. "I was afraid you wouldn't come."

"I considered passing right by," he said, trying to be witty, "but I have to have my coffee."

She smiled. There it was again, that smile. Matt really wished she wouldn't look at him so sadly.

She laced her fingers together. "Okay, I didn't look him up, so I'm not sure who this Doctor Smith is – "

"E.E. 'Doc' Smith," he corrected.

Wait.

His eyes widened.

"A writer, I'm guessing? 'Clear ether' was your quote. With an exclamation point."

He stared another moment, the coffee shop slowly fading from existence around him. He no longer heard the hissing of the espresso machine or the din of voices. He no longer felt the hard chair underneath him or the cold glass table top under his forearms. The only sight in focus was the pair of chocolate eyes looking back at him, watching him, waiting.

"You used a darker pen than usual," she added.

He closed his eyes for a moment, his thoughts chasing and tumbling over one another, all racing headlong to an unthinkable conclusion he couldn't steer away from: he believed her.

He opened his eyes in time to see a wave of relief pass over her face.

He cleared his suddenly dry throat, tried remembering everything she had tried to tell him the night before about Jenny when he had only been half-listening.

"What's going to happen to . . . her?" He could hardly find his voice. For a moment, he thought he might not have spoken loud enough for her to hear him.

"I don't know exactly," she said. "That's why I'm here."

"Can you . . . can't you keep whatever happens from happening? Can't you take control and . . ." He stopped talking. She was shaking her head.

"I'm here to observe. Just observe. Please, Matt. I need you to just go to work and keep to your normal routine."

He rubbed his scrunched forehead.

"Then why . . . why did you come to my house? You wanted me to help you stop it, right?" He leaned across the table. His heartbeat and breathing seemed too fast, too noticeable. He pressed a hand against his chest. "Why did you tell me about this, make me believe that this is really, truly happening, that what you can do is a thing that could be done, and then ask me not to do anything?"

"I made a mistake." Her chin quivered slightly. She reached her hand toward his, seemed to change her mind, pulled it back. "It isn't fair. It's all my fault, and I apologize, but you can't do anything, Matt. Promise me."

He stared, noticed he had balled his hands into fists.

He forced himself to lean back in his chair, let his gaze drift around the crowded shop before returning and focusing his gaze on her. "Tell me who you really are."

"I can't."

"Give me a name."

She shook her head again, this time decidedly.

"Helping Jenny is the only thing that matters. Now, go get your coffee as you normally would while I let Jenny return." She waited. He waited as well, for his breathing to settle, for his heartbeat to quiet. Finally, he gave her a small nod. "Remember, Jenny isn't consciously aware of me. You can't tell her anything. You can't tell anyone anything."

He nodded a second time, pushed himself up from the table, scraping the chair against the floor. He let his gaze linger on her face. Except, she wasn't Jenny. Jenny's face wasn't her real face.

He sighed. "Will I talk to you again, before . . . well . . . whatever happens?"

"I don't think so," she said.

Such sorrow in those eyes, as if she were grieving.

Just like the night before, a chill ran through him.

"Well, this could be goodbye, then."

"Goodbye, Matt."

He turned away.

He stepped into line, ordered his usual, and waited for his name to be called, keeping his gaze focused forward and away from the table. He didn't want to see the transformation take place.

"Large Americano, lightly sweetened, for Matt."

"Thank you."

He retrieved his drink and turned to leave, took a few tentative steps, but couldn't keep himself from looking back at Jenny's table.

Jenny Coulter sat with her hands curled around her coffee cup, her gaze focused on the laptop now sitting open in front of her. He couldn't see the entire screen from his vantagepoint, but she appeared to be looking through email. Yes, this was the Jenny he sort-of knew, the one he had seen in passing at the office. *Not Jenny* had retreated. Real Jenny was in control.

Something would happen today, something so upsetting that Jenny would need *Not Jenny*'s help to recover from it. Matt pictured her frightened face from the night before, couldn't imagine what she would be going through soon, how horrific the imminent event would be.

Poor Jenny. Poor Jenny. The thought repeated on a loop in his head.

Real Jenny suddenly looked up at him.

He had stood there too long, staring at her.

"Matt," she said. There was a soft question mark at the end of his name. She pointed at him. "You were in my . . . I mean . . . never mind."

He swallowed. Was she talking about her "dream"? He had to ignore that statement. He couldn't have her trying to remember any details.

"Good morning," he said. He tried to smile, thought he accomplished it. "Come here often?"

She nodded. "I'm here every morning."

Every morning. He lifted his eyebrows.

"Oh, me too. Then we've probably been here at the same time before. If so, I hope you didn't think I was ignoring you."

The corner of her mouth turned up slightly. She shook her head.

Matt heard *Not Jenny*'s warnings in his head. He shouldn't linger. He should go to work. He had promised.

"The quarterly slides are due today, right?"

"Yes." She glanced toward her laptop, turned back to him. "Would you like some help? The new format is a bit confusing."

The steam from his cup caught his eye and he watched it for the briefest of seconds. Getting help from Jenny, who handled all the training materials and quarterly and annual reports for their department, couldn't do any harm. It was a natural, work-related activity.

"I would, actually, if you have the time."

"All right." She stood. "If you want, email your file to me and come by my desk. I'm over near the server room. I'm going to get a refill to go and then we can walk in together."

"Great!"

Jenny stood to join the line and Matt took a sip of his Americano, wondering if he was capable of keeping his promise, wishing that he had ordered an extra shot of espresso.

By the time he left her desk, Matt relearned two things he already knew: never leave a presentation to the last minute, and Jenny Coulter was hard to get to know. During the hour they spent together, she answered his personal queries with polite but short replies before immediately turning the conversation back to business. Did she have any pets? Yes. Always know your audience. Did she plan to attend the company picnic? Maybe. Know your story and keep control of its pace. Did she like science-fiction? Some. Don't use that chart; the metrics aren't clear.

But he also learned that Jenny knew her stuff, and even a lot of his.

She reworded his long sentences into clear, concise statements, adding points he had forgotten, replaced jargon with simpler, straightforward terms, and rearranged and animated the slides to convey a clearer message with a controlled pace. When they were both satisfied, she saved the file and emailed it back to him.

"That was impressive, Jenny. Thank you."

"You're welcome," she said. She stood and gathered a notebook and pen from her desk.

"Now, I have to go to my first meeting."

"Oh, right."

He stepped out of her way and he thought she flashed him a small smile as she passed him. He watched her until she disappeared down the hall.

Would it happen here at work? During lunch?

Not Jenny had asked for the impossible from him. How could he just forget about it?

He returned to his desk, opened his email and forwarded the presentation to his boss, crediting Jenny for her excellent help. Then he added her as a contact in the chat app on his phone.

Meetings, phone calls, email, instant chats, text messages – all seemed suddenly, and infuriatingly, boring. He drummed his fingers on his desk long and loud enough to be yelled at by his neighbor on the other side of the cubicle divider. He thought he caught a glimpse of Jenny rounding a corner, but otherwise he didn't have a chance to talk to her again. And what would he say to her if he did? He had made a promise not to interfere, he reminded himself, albeit with the slightest nod of his head.

5:55. The work day was finally over. As far as Matt could tell, everyone else had left. Phones had stopped ringing, printers had stopped printing, conversations had ceased, most of the motion sensor lights had switched off. As usual, he would be the last one to leave, at 6:00 on the dot.

Matt packed his laptop, slipped his backpack over his shoulder, and headed toward the side door, taking a route past the server room so he could make sure everything was locked up tight. It would also take him past Jenny's cubicle.

She wasn't there. Her chair was pushed in neatly under her desk. He didn't see her raincoat or her bag or her backpack. Her laptop was gone as well.

Matt swallowed.

So, that was it then. He would just go home. Maybe he wouldn't even find out what had happened until he came in the next day to see his coworkers gathered at her cubicle, expressing disbelief and sympathy. Would it happen on her way home?

Jenny had left her umbrella. A thunderclap

rattled the windows just as he laid eyes on it. It stood propped up in the corner of her cubicle behind the coat rack. His heart began to race. Maybe he could catch her, offer to walk her home. Wasn't it the least he could do, after she'd spent so much time helping him?

He snatched up the umbrella and headed for the side door, pushed it open.

"Jen – !"

Someone grabbed him from behind and put a hand over his mouth, wrenching his left arm up behind his back.

He let out a startled, muffled cry of pain.

"Right on time, aren't you, Matt?" A voice rumbled near his ear. He didn't recognize it.

With a strong, persistent shove, he was pushed back inside and up against the server room door, his face pressed up against the access panel. He dropped the umbrella.

"Open it."

Matt could hardly breathe. He reached up with his free hand, for a split second considered resisting, then entered the 8-digit code. The server room lock popped open. The man holding him shoved him forward, then stuck his foot out to flip down the doorstop.

"Thanks," the rumbling voice sneered.

A blazing pain shot through the base of his skull.

Matt staggered and slumped to the floor, his eyes closed shut against throbbing pain. His head dropped onto the cold, raised flooring. He heard the whirr of disk drives, the droning hum of fluorescent lights. He sensed someone stepping over him, once, then a second time, or maybe it was a second person, and then he heard fainter footsteps and rustling coming from the server racks.

This could be it, Jenny's incident, the cause of her trauma. She must be coming back, to get her umbrella maybe. She might hear the voices, come to investigate.

He no longer cared about his promise. He had to warn her.

He fumbled his phone out of his pocket, managed to open one eye, found the now blurry chat app icon, and pressed it. Jenny's name came up first as the most recently added.

stayout148

He wanted to add an exclamation point but his hands were starting to shake and he pressed send instead. He hoped Jenny knew

148 was the server room's room number.

He let his arm drop to the floor by his side.

If the thieves returned, he would close his eyes and maybe they would ignore him. On the other hand, he was afraid he might not be able to open them again.

He waited, glanced at his phone in case she replied, afraid she might call instead. Nothing. But that was good. If she stayed out of the room, whatever the reason, that would be good.

The fire alarm started screaming.

What? An actual fire, or had someone discovered the break-in? He couldn't move. He covered his ears to block the deafening, relentless claxon.

He heard yelling. Two men carrying boxes ran past him out of the room, yelling to one another. "Go. Leave him. Go!"

He closed his eyes tightly, wishing the claxon would stop, wishing his head would stop pounding.

"Matt. Matt!"

He opened the one eye he could manage.

Jenny's face resolved in front of him.

"Is it you?" he said, or thought he said. He wasn't sure if he had actually spoken or not.

"Yes, it's me, Jenny. I got your chat. I didn't know what to do so I pulled the fire alarm."

He blinked his eyes until they cleared and he stared into her eyes. The dark eyes he stared into now were clearly Jenny's. Kind, concerned, anxious. But she didn't look at him quite the same way *Not Jenny* had, with nostalgic familiarity.

"You've been hit on the head. You're bleeding."

Matt heard the words. He thought he understood them.

"Help is coming."

He couldn't nod. He could barely speak. Instead, he blinked slowly in acknowledgment.

In the year that followed, Matt nearly convinced himself more than once that the 'consciousness from the future' had been a product of his imagination. He had suffered a severe head wound after all, and his memory could have been affected, scrambling his perception of reality. But each time he questioned *Not Jenny*'s existence, he would open his journal to that day's entry, the day when the very different Jenny Coulter had appeared on his stoop in the rain, and he re-read the quote he had written in dark blue ink, and he could think of no other explanation. So, he invariably concluded *Not Jenny* had been real, and, following that, its corollary: the timeline had changed.

Jenny had been upset by what happened in the server room, but not to the extent *Not Jenny* had described. She took a short leave, but as far as Matt could tell, hadn't suffered any long-term effects. Either *Not Jenny* had been wrong, or lied, or something had changed. If it was the latter, he suspected he was the cause.

Occasionally, when Matt met Jenny's gaze, he caught himself looking for *Not Jenny* behind her eyes, as if he expected she might be a silent passenger in Jenny's mind again, but then he would scold himself. If *Not Jenny* was inhabiting her mind, that would mean they hadn't saved Jenny from trauma after all, and he certainly didn't want that. He liked Jenny. In fact, they had become pretty friendly since their shared experience. They even started working on projects together, often meeting at *The Perfect Grind* in the mornings to prepare presentations and reports.

He wrote to *Not Jenny* in his journal, hoping the act would satisfy a yearning he couldn't explain, and found, to his surprise, that the words came easily. He used the darker ink so she would know it was meant for her. He recounted what Jenny had told him, and the police, about receiving his chat, pulling the alarm, and seeing two men running from the server room before finding Matt inside. The two men, hired by a rival company, had stolen backup disks containing proprietary company data. Luckily, the thieves had been caught in time, along with their mole, a new part-timer who had shared information about Matt's server access and his dependable habits.

Matt also told her how he thought of her whenever it rained.

And then, late one evening, almost three months after the incident in the server room, he stopped writing.

The realization dawned on him midsentence, his pen lifting itself up off the page. She would never read what he was so diligently writing. She wouldn't be reading his journal because she would no longer have access to it, because investigators only looked through people's journals if they had gone missing . . . died. If he had died in the original timeline, if Jenny had seen it happen, that would explain her trauma. It would explain *Not Jenny*'s sad eyes and bittersweet smile.

Matt's stomach churned. Everyone knew, intellectually, that each day could be their last. Anything could happen. Simple decisions could make the difference between life and death – turning left instead of right, crossing the street, taking a later flight. But this was not hypothetical. He knew another timeline had once existed where he had died on the server room floor.

His fingers trembled when he put the dark pen and the journal into his desk drawer and locked it away.

The days crawled by.

Most people, he wagered, would be inspired by a brush with death to pack their days with significance and memory-making moments with friends and family, but Matt found it hard to socialize. He felt as if time had been suspended, as if he was waiting for something to happen to restart the clock.

He stayed home most evenings, and treated himself to pizza on Fridays, and sometimes Saturdays, and on "special" occasions, like today, when he needed comfort food.

The doorbell rang. The pizza had arrived.

Matt pulled out his wallet as he opened the door.

He recognized the girl standing in front of him. She brought his pizza every Friday. Young, probably just old enough to drive, wisps of blonde hair escaping her knit cap. She had bright, blue eyes and pale skin offset by ruddy cheeks.

"Hi, Mr. James." She handed him the box and he set it on the small table by the door. "It's $17.75 tonight."

"Okay, sure." He rifled through the small bills in his wallet, trying to count them quickly. "Wait, I think I have a twenty in the other room."

She nodded.

He turned and went to his bedroom and pulled a twenty out of the front pocket of the jeans he had thrown onto the bed, then returned to the girl waiting for him by the door, his arm outstretched.

"Here you go."

"Thank you."

The girl took the bill from him, then her arm dropped abruptly to her side. Her expression faded. Her gaze lost focus. For a frightening second, he thought she might have stopped breathing, before she finally drew in an audible breath and turned to look at him again.

Matt swallowed.

Her smile reappeared, only it looked different somehow. "How have you been, Matt?"

Something in her tone, her stance, her expression, summoned his gaze to meet hers.

He knew the pizza girl. He saw her every week, sometimes twice. She was familiar. But in this moment, she seemed familiar in a different way.

Her gaze drifted to the bookshelves behind him, scanned them for a moment, and then returned to him. "By the Talyst, you have a lot of books!"

"What did you just say?" His breath caught in his lungs. "Did you say 'by the Talyst'?"

When she nodded, he took a step back. "How do you know that phrase?"

She opened her mouth to answer, but he continued before she had a chance to reply.

"That's a phrase I came up with for a sci-fi novel I planned to write someday." His heart pounded. "I only told one person about it--a man named Elliott, my grandfather's roommate from the nursing home."

They had become good buddies, he and Elliott, talking for hours one evening after his grandfather had fallen asleep. He had shared most of his life story, including his silly dream of becoming a writer. That had been the night before the fire in the rec room. He'd heard Elliott had started it, that the guilt had been overwhelming. One might have said he had experienced a trauma.

"Is it you? *Not Jenny*?" This girl's blue eyes looked so different from Jenny's milk-chocolate ones, yet Matt could still sense *Not Jenny* behind them. "Were you observing Elliott? Is this poor girl about to experience some kind of trauma?"

The flush in the girl's cheeks drained away. Her voice cracked. "How do you know all this?"

"You told me. You told me who you are, when you are, that you're some kind of a 'time sensor' person, that you were here observing Jenny. You told me not to interfere, but somehow I must have because . . . "

His words stopped coming. Once again, realization stopped him in mid-sentence.

Jenny hadn't been traumatized. He hadn't died. *Not Jenny* wouldn't have had anything to investigate.

"You don't remember," he said. His mouth finally allowed words to form again, but they came slowly. "You can't remember. For you, it never happened."

The girl's wide eyes pierced right through him. She drew in a long, unsteady breath.

"Are you saying that I took control of a client, revealed myself to you, and changed the timeline?" Her voice pitched up into soprano range. "Why would I do that?"

He swallowed. "I think I died in that original timeline. I think you just wanted to . . . well . . . tell me goodbye."

The girl covered her mouth with her hand, the twenty-dollar bill still clutched between her fourth finger and her pinky. She scrunched her forehead, as if her head suddenly ached. Then she nodded, not so much to him as to herself.

She dropped her hand, sighed. "Elliott liked listening to your stories. He liked you quite a bit, in fact. I liked you, too. Too much, it seems." She gave him a small smile. "I must have done what I'm doing now, taking control just to spend another moment with you."

Matt reached out to her., his fingertips just brushing the sleeve of her jacket. "Look, why don't you come inside and we can talk some more? Maybe we can make a plan to meet up. I can meet the real you."

"I can't," she said.

"Oh, right, of course." He gave the pizza girl's body an encompassing look. "But later, come and find me. You know where I live, after all!"

She smiled. He liked *Not Jenny*'s smile, no

matter whose face was wearing it. He hated to see it fade away.

"I don't know that I can. I'm not exactly free to do as I please. But I'll try." She paused. "It may be a long wait for you, though."

"I'll wait," he said.

She smiled. "Then I promise I'll try my best. I really do want to find out more about the Talyst. But for now, I need to retreat." She lifted her arm and reached out to him, pushed the twenty back into his hand. "Pay her for the pizza."

He nodded. He couldn't seem to think of anything else to say, except for,

"Clear ether," he said.

"What?"

He smiled. "Safe travel."

She nodded. "Goodbye, Matt."

He watched her go. The young girl's expression fell blank for an instant, and then a bright, but very different light, returned to her eyes.

She held out her hand, and once again, for the first time, he handed her the twenty.

"Thanks! See you Friday," she said. She

bounded down off his stoop.

Matt stepped down to the sidewalk as the girl's motorcycle roared away down the street, stood staring long after the taillights had disappeared.

He might have years to wait, but he would meet *Not Jenny* again. He felt certain. Until then, he had a pizza to devour, all six books of E.E. "Doc" Smith's Lensman Series to re-read, new entries to add to his journal, and a sci-fi novel waiting to be written. He smiled, glanced down at his watch. It was still early evening.

He had plenty of time.

Ann Bernath

Ann Bernath

When You Were
Not Jenny
Again

ANN BERNATH

Tom –

Thank you for demanding a follow-up to
"When You Were *Not Jenny.*"

This wouldn't exist without you.

Ann Bernath

When You Were
Not Jenny
Again

Ann Bernath

"**Y**ou're doing it again," Jenny said.

Matt tore his gaze from Jenny's milk-chocolate eyes and blinked, bringing her face into focus.

"What am I doing again?"

"Looking at me . . . that way." She pursed her lips. "If I didn't know better I'd think you liked me, but that sad face tells me that isn't true. What are you thinking about exactly? Do

I remind you of someone?"

He hadn't intended to stare. He never intended to. But when she looked at him a certain way, the way she must have just then when she lifted her gaze to look at him over her laptop monitor, her eyes always drew him in. He admitted that at the beginning, immediately after the timeline changed, he had purposefully searched Jenny's eyes, hoping to find *Not Jenny* behind them, but a year had passed since then. He thought he had succeeded in convincing himself that he would never find *Not Jenny* behind her eyes again, but, apparently, his subconscious still believed otherwise.

"I'm sorry," he said. "I swear I don't realize I'm doing it. I can't explain why."

He could, of course, explain why, but Jenny would never believe him. She didn't know there had been a timeline when he'd died. She didn't know that a girl from the future had possessed her traumatized mind through her memories and changed everything. How could he explain that?

Jenny shook her head, smiled. "Fine. I forgive you. As long as you know that I'm going to keep calling you out when you do it. Also, you should know that I'm dating Bobby

Flynn now."

"Bobby? You mean *Detective* Flynn? The one who investigated the break in?"

She smiled. "Yes. Detective Robert Flynn. Since the case closed a year ago, he felt clear to give me a call." She dropped her gaze and smiled, as if reliving a recent, romantic memory, then looked back up again. "When you invited me over, you promised me a pizza."

"Did I?"

"You said you always have pizza on Friday nights, and here it is, Friday night, and I'm not helping you out on this presentation for free."

"All right." Matt stood. "A promise is a promise. I'll go get a pizza. Extra large?"

"You're going to go get it? But it's raining, and you always have it delivered."

"Yes, well, I need to stretch. I'll grab a couple six-packs while I'm out, too. I'm running low."

"OK. Get the usual then, and remember to keep the mushrooms on your half. And don't buy cheap beer this time."

"Got it."

Matt grabbed his coat from the coat rack, assured himself that he had his wallet and that his car keys jangled in the inside pocket of his coat, then went out the front door onto the stoop. He slipped into his coat and pulled the hood up just as raindrops dripped off the eaves and the brisk air sought his exposed neck.

Angelenos didn't like driving in the rain. He doubted that many would go out on a night like this if they could get delivery, so he was grateful that Jenny hadn't questioned him further. He didn't want to make up more excuses. He didn't want to tell her that he was afraid if he opened the door and saw the pizza girl standing there, he might search her eyes the same way he searched Jenny's.

The roads were packed proving Matt had been wrong about people not wanting to go out. Drivers unused to rain and slick roads were either driving too fast or frustratingly slow. When he found a space along the curb in front of *Pete's-a-Pie,* he parked and sighed in relief.

His cell phone rang.

"Hey, Jenny."

"Matt, did you order delivery anyway?"

"No. Why?"

"Because there's a girl at the door who's

telling me she's the pizza girl. Except . . . she doesn't actually *have* a pizza that I can see. She says she needs to talk to you. Do you owe her money or something?"

Matt's heart pounded a heavy stroke.

"She's still there? Does she look normal?"

"Normal? What do you mean? How should I know?"

Matt released the parking brake, started the engine. "Invite her in. Keep her there. I'm coming back."

"But, do you have the pizza?"

"No. We'll order delivery. Just keep her there."

He reinserted himself into traffic.

Could it be her? Was she possessing the pizza girl again? Just a week before she had controlled the girl to talk to him and had told him that it would be a long time before she talked to him again.

If it really was her, the girl from the future he called *Not Jenny,* she could only take control of a possessed mind and body for so long. At least, that's what she told him that first night when she appeared at his door, possessing Jenny, on a rainy night like tonight.

If he didn't hurry he might lose his chance

to talk to her again.

But even as he parked and ran to his front door, exhaling in visible puffs, he knew he had missed her. He knew he had taken too long. Damn the traffic.

Matt stopped in the kitchen doorway, catching his breath, reluctant to enter, for Jenny hadn't even looked up when he came in, even though he had slammed the door shut behind him. She sat alone at the table where he'd left her, sitting sideways in her chair, staring at the kitchen window's closed curtains, wearing a look Matt had learned to know well. Something had happened that Jenny was processing.

He dropped into the chair across from her and waited what felt like a long moment before she spoke.

"She's gone," she said. She turned toward him and pushed her phone across the table. "She left you a message. I told her we could just call you, but she said something about running out of time."

Time. Yes, it was all about time.

He picked the phone up and touched the screen to wake it, then stared at the frozen image of the blue-eyed, blonde pizza girl staring back at him, knowing that he could be setting himself up for disappointment. It could really just be the pizza girl telling him he'd shortchanged her and she had come to collect.

He touched the play icon.

"Hello, Matt."

His heart responded to her voice.

It was her. *Not Jenny*. Even though this was the pizza girl's voice, the same voice that he heard every Friday when she brought his order, she had spoken his name now the same way *Not Jenny* always did, with bittersweet familiarity. Happy to see him. Sad to see him.

"I hoped I would get to see you again in person, but this might be better in the long run. This way I can say everything I need to say without the distraction of looking into your sweet face." The pizza girl smiled, straightened, then placed her forefinger on her chest. "This is Sophie. Sometime soon, in your present, she'll suffer an incident that will cause her to wander for days with no memory of what happened to her. Since no one knows the exact day or time, I've been dropping into various days in her memory. The first day was the last time she brought you your pizza, when I couldn't help myself and took control just to tell you hello. That's when you told me about

Jenny and the timeline we changed and I've been thinking about it ever since."

Matt glanced over at Jenny. She would have heard all of this as it was recorded, but even hearing it a second time, it must still sound like crazy nonsense to her.

"Matt. I have two favors to ask of you, if you're willing." She stabbed at her chest with her forefinger. "Sophie's parents have exhausted their savings and can't pay for my services any longer, so I'm being taken off her case. But I don't want to abandon her, so after what you told me about changing your timeline, I've been thinking maybe we can change Sophie's timeline too."

She leaned closer to the phone, her eyes wide and pleading.

"Can you follow her? Maybe you can intervene somehow? Like I said, no one knows when it happened – will happen – but I heard her mumbling something about not wanting to pull a Saturday shift, so maybe it happens as soon as your tomorrow? It's a lot to ask, but it's all I can do for her now. " She held up an envelope. "The other favor is much simpler. I used Sophie to write a letter to Elliott's daughter. Can you deliver it for me?"

She gazed into the phone's camera and

smiled, and Matt cursed the traffic again. He had missed the chance to search behind those eyes to feel near her again.

"I have to say goodbye now. I can't interrupt Sophie's day too much or she'll realize she's lost time. Please save Sophie if you can, but no matter what you decide, I do hope I get to meet you as me sometime. Goodbye, Matt."

The image moved from the pizza girl to the ceiling.

"Here's your phone. Thank you. You're Matt's coworker Jenny, right? Jenny Flynn? Oh, wait. Not yet. Sorry. Sometimes I can't keep the sequence of events straight."

The video ended.

Matt released his tight grip on the phone and laid it on the table, grabbed his face with both hands, his heart racing.

"Matt."

He looked up. Jenny, her arms crossed over her chest, was leaning back in her chair, her eyebrows lifted.

"Do you want to explain?"

"You won't believe me."

"You can't be sure of that. I've been sitting here trying to come to grips with the fact that she called me Jenny Flynn. *You* didn't even know we were dating. How could she know about Bobby? Plus, I watched your reaction just now. You looked like a forlorn puppy, but nothing she said surprised you." She tapped the envelope that sat next to her keyboard, the one *Not Jenny* had held up in the video. "I don't understand any of it, but I can go with you to deliver this letter. That seems straightforward enough. As for following the pizza girl, I don't think that's something you should do alone. You'll need help, and if not me, who else would you ask?"

Jenny Coulter, who according to *Not Jenny* would someday marry the detective and become Jenny Flynn, was too smart for him. Matt couldn't get away with anything but the truth now. Even if she didn't believe everything, someone needed saving. If nothing else, Jenny could believe that.

"We'll need beer," Matt said.

*N*ot Jenny, Matt explained, had described herself as a Temporal Empathic Sensor. She had the ability to enter a person's past through their memories, most of the time observing, but for brief periods could take control of that person's consciousness. In the original timeline, Matt had died in the server room break-in, and Jenny had been too traumatized to describe what happened, her weakened state of mind enabling *Not Jenny* to enter her past to observe, and only observe, the incident. But she had broken her own rules, taking control of Jenny's mind so she could say hello, and goodbye, to Matt. She hadn't intended to tell him anything at all, but she had ultimately revealed herself. Somehow, his foreknowledge had altered his actions enough that the timeline changed. He lived, Jenny didn't experience the trauma, and when *Not Jenny* visited Matt as the pizza girl, she didn't remember helping Jenny at all. For her, none of it had happened.

Matt took a long swig of his beer.

It all still sounded like nonsense, no matter how carefully he tried to explain it.

Jenny sat on his couch. He sat in his recliner. His last six-pack, dwindled now to three cans, sat on the coffee table between them. Matt drank directly from the can. Jenny preferred a glass.

Jenny sat for a time without speaking, taking small sips of her beer, staring at the foam. When she finally looked over the rim of her glass at him, her brow was furrowed.

"Why did she break the rules to tell you hello and goodbye? Did you two know each other before that?"

"Well, I didn't know *her* then. You heard her mention Elliott's daughter in the video? She's referring to the daughter of my grandfather's friend from the nursing home. I think her name is Susan. Elliott and I used to talk a lot. I talked his ear off, I think. I told him about my writing aspirations and the good times with my grandfather growing up. We became friends. She was just observing, but I guess she got to know me through him."

"Whoever she is, she seems quite fond of you." Jenny's voice was soft.

Matt smiled, nodded. "I guess so."

He knew it was strange, even under normal circumstances, to make such a connection so quickly. Perhaps it was the flush of excitement or because the circumstances weren't anywhere close to normal that he formed such a strong and deep bond. Perhaps it was the way she spoke or the way she looked at him or her very aura that he yearned for long after she told him goodbye. Even in a video message, speaking to him through another person, he could still feel that connection.

He sighed, aware that Jenny was waiting for him to continue.

"I became quite fond of her, too, when she talked to me through you."

"Ah." Jenny leaned back against the couch cushions. "That explains all the soul searching looks you've been giving me. I *do* remind you of someone."

Matt set his can of beer on the coffee table.

"Wait. Are you saying you believe me?"

"I'd rather not, to be honest, because my rational self is screaming at me right now. But I can't make anything make sense otherwise. Not to mention that I can't forget the dream I had the night before the break-in where I was suddenly standing in this very living room where I'd never been before, and yet every detail I remember from that dream is real. The layout, the furniture, the books, the records. It wasn't a dream, was it? *She* brought me here when she possessed me, didn't she?" When Matt nodded, she continued. "Then, the morning of the break-in, I thought I had fallen asleep in the coffee shop before you suddenly showed up and we walked to work together, but that always felt odd because I have trouble falling asleep in my own bed let alone sitting on one of those hard chairs at *The Perfect Grind*. She had taken control then too, right?"

"Yes."

Jenny blew air between her lips. "Well, my brain is doing cartwheels."

She resumed drinking, in large gulps now, her expression signaling that her mind was once again processing.

"Alright," she said. "For now I can ignore my brain while it sorts itself out. In the meantime, you can tell me how I can help you do what she's asked you to do, because my chest is tight thinking that we're wasting time here when we could be saving that girl."

Matt smiled. He and Jenny hadn't known each other very well before the break-in, but they had become friends in the year since. Not only had he lived, but he had gained an important person in his life.

"Jenny Coulter, soon to be Flynn, I think you're my best friend."

"I know I am," she said. She looked to her left then her right then turned back and grinned. "I don't see anybody else here."

T he Sunnyside Retirement Home sat nestled at the end of a pleasant cul-de-sac against the foothills of the San Gabriel Mountains. The recreation building by the pool had been rebuilt after the fire, the fire that Elliott Barnes thought he started with an unextinguished cigarette two years ago, a mere month after Matt's grandfather had passed away. Elliott still resided at Sunnyside, except now instead of the kind and jovial man whose face lit up when Matt entered the room, he suffered from depression. His daughter Susan visited him daily, but according to the staff, Elliott withdrew more every day, and Susan was at her wit's end.

"So, Matt." Jenny hurried beside Matt's long strides down the main pathway between Sunnyside's main entrance and Elliott's bungalow. "You said that girl from the future will soon be helping Elliott *now* and meeting you *back then*?"

"Yeah. Kind of crazy to think about, huh?"

Jenny nodded, then shook her head. "Just so you know, I'm fully prepared to learn that all of this is just an elaborate prank at my expense."

He shot her a smile. "Noted."

They found Susan sitting in a chair at Elliott's bedside, a book in her hands.

Elliott lay on a normal, twin-sized bed, his head and back propped up with pillows. Matt had expected to see him in a hospital bed like the one his grandfather had used, but Elliott's problems didn't appear to require one. He was dressed in matching sweat pants and sweatshirt, a tray of half-eaten food sitting on the bed beside him. He didn't turn his head when Matt and Jenny entered. Instead, he continued to stare out his bedroom window.

Matt stepped forward and extended his hand to Susan.

"Hello, Susan, isn't it? I'm Matt James. Your father might have mentioned me? This is my friend Jenny Coulter."

Susan appeared to be in her sixties, her short, dark hair obviously dyed judging by the gray roots showing on the top of her head. She closed her book and moved to rise but Matt waved her back down.

She took his hand and squeezed it.

"Matt! Yes, hello. Dad talks about you all the time, when he isn't staring out the window." She pointed to a small couch nearby. "Won't you sit down?"

17

"Thank you, but no, we just stopped by to give you a letter."

Matt pulled the envelope *Not Jenny* – or maybe he should refer to her as *Not Sophie* now – had entrusted to him from his jacket pocket and handed it to her.

"A letter? Who would be sending me a letter?"

"A friend of my grandfather's," Matt said. He had thought of other possible explanations, but decided this was the simplest and the closest to the truth.

Susan opened the envelope and withdrew two handwritten pages, unfolded them, and scanned the opening paragraphs.

Matt admitted that he had been tempted to read it. *Not Jenny* had written it, after all. But he hadn't touched it, even though his mind tried to coerce him into believing that the letter had weight and heat and should be removed from his pocket. He felt a sense of relief now that he had turned the letter over without succumbing, but its absence pricked at his heart.

Susan looked up. "Before you go, Matt, can I ask a favor? I'd like to add you as a secondary emergency contact for Dad."

Matt nodded. "All right. That's fine."

"Here." Susan picked up a pen from the nightstand next to Elliott's bed. "Maybe you can just write your address here on this envelope."

Matt took the pen and envelope and wrote his name and address, surprised that he needed to wipe away a niggling, stinging sensation in his eyes with the back of his hand before handing both items back to her.

"Thank you so much," Susan said.

Jenny put a hand on his shoulder. "Come on, Matt. We have another favor that needs doing."

He nodded. Yes. They had to go save Sophie. They couldn't stay here and wait. He had no way of knowing when *Not Jenny* would come to sit with Elliott. He had considered asking Susan if she had already hired or planned to hire an unconventional treatment for her father, hoping to ascertain how soon *Not Jenny* would come, but he'd talked himself out of it. Just asking the question could jeopardize their meeting in the past. He couldn't risk that.

Matt nodded to Jenny. "Right. Let's go. Nice to meet you, Susan." Matt turned and placed his hand over Elliott's arthritic fingers, thought he saw a flicker of recognition in the old man's milky eyes. "Take care, Elliott. And don't worry. Everything will be fine."

Detective Robert Flynn insisted under no uncertain terms that he would not only accompany Matt and Jenny to follow Sophie, but that he would drive and they would take his unmarked police car. It was too dangerous for two civilians to pursue a stalker, and why hadn't Sophie filed a report with the police? Matt explained that Sophie had been reluctant to do so since she only had a gut feeling rather than hard evidence.

Matt hated to perpetuate Jenny's fabrication, but he agreed with her that it only made sense to enlist a professional.

"So, you're telling me this pizza place only deals in cash?" Flynn navigated between lanes following Sophie's motorcycle, keeping her taillights in sight without driving too close behind her. "I guess if they aren't a chain, it's more economical that way, but it's riskier for the deliverers."

Jenny rode up front in the passenger seat while Matt sat in the back leaning to one side to see out the front window between them.

"Thanks for helping out, Detective," Matt said.

"No problem. I'm used to long stakeouts. The trick is to keep boredom from dulling your senses."

Matt nodded. They had been following Sophie for hours now as she made delivery after delivery, traveling back and forth between her customer's houses and *Pete's-a-Pie*, assessing the cars around her on the road, scanning the neighborhood's sidewalks as well as the customers themselves as they opened their doors to receive their orders. As the hour neared midnight and Sophie emerged from the restaurant once again carrying an order, Jenny turned to look back at Matt and they exchanged nervous, lifted eyebrows. Either they were about to waste the detective's time and would need to try again another night, or something would be happening soon.

While they sat parked in front of the restaurant, Matt slumping in the back seat in case Sophie were to look in their direction and recognize him, Sophie secured the insulated pizza bag to her motorcycle's rear luggage rack.

An apron-clad man stepped out of the restaurant's front doors and shouted to her.

"Last delivery, Sophie. You can go on home after. See you next week."

Sophie lifted her arm and waved in response, and the man stepped back inside.

"This could be it," Matt said. He whispered it, even though he doubted anyone outside the car would hear him.

"Yes," Flynn said. "If the stalker is going to make a move, this would be a good time since she isn't expected to return."

Again they followed her, up until and after her delivery, keeping a car between them, then both a motorcycle and a car behind when traffic stopped at a light before crossing a two-lane bridge.

Jenny pointed. "That other motorcycle pulled up alongside her. Are they talking?"

Flynn edged the car forward, following the car in front of them who had drifted forward to close the gap.

"Could be," he said. He straightened in his seat and turned his police radio on, preparing, Matt assumed, just in case. "There are two riders on that bike. Only one has a helmet. They look like they're arguing. Well, your friend seems to be arguing with them. The two on the other bike look like they're taunting her."

The light turned green. The two

motorcycles sped forward, the one with two riders attempting to outrun Sophie's, and when they came to the first side street, the two motorcycles leaned their bikes around the corner and disappeared.

"Where'd they go?"

Flynn braked and followed them, Matt just catching a glimpse of the two pairs of motorcycle taillights entering a pedestrian bridge that crossed back over the river. As they drew closer, he saw the bikes emerge on the opposite side and drop onto the paved bicycle and hiking trail that ran along the length of the waterway.

"Damn."

Flynn pulled the car over next to the pedestrian bridge. The bridge was paved but a large stone post in the middle of the path blocked vehicles from entering. Pedestrians and bicycles could easily navigate around it, and, although legally prohibited according to the warning sign, motorcycles could squeeze around the post as well.

"Do you see them?" Flynn turned around in his seat.

Matt shook his head. The streetlights that illuminated the trail flickered, a sign of aging bulbs or faulty wiring, making it difficult to see, but then the roar of two engines preceded the headlights of two motorcycles riding single file returning the way they had come. They crossed the bridge, swerved around the post, and sped out onto the street.

Two motorcycles. Two riders.

"That one's Sophie's bike, but that's not Sophie," Jenny said. She unlocked her passenger door. "Bobby, go on. Matt and I will go look for her."

"Be careful. Take this flashlight. I'll follow those two and call for backup," he said.

Matt grabbed his own flashlight and he and Jenny exited the car. As Flynn pulled away, Matt saw him open his driver side window and place his siren on the car's roof where it began to wail and flash its swirling lights.

Matt and Jenny crossed the bridge and reached the trail, one looking left, the other right, scanning ahead of them as well as the river bed below. They walked as close to the edge as they could without risking a tumble over the rocks that had been cemented into place to form the river's steep bank. The river was often dry, but not today, not after the days of steady rain the southland had experienced over the previous week.

"There!"

Matt spotted her. Sophie was lying face down at the river's edge, water lapping up onto her face as it streamed by. She no longer wore her helmet, nor did Matt see it nearby. The rider they had seen without a helmet must have taken it when he took her bike, then pushed her down the embankment.

Matt and Jenny scrambled down over the rocks to reach her.

She looked deathly pale. Her head was bleeding. She was unconscious, but she was breathing steadily. Matt thought about pulling her away from the water but decided he shouldn't move her. As long as she wouldn't drown, she was in no immediate danger remaining where she lay.

Matt called 911.

"She's so . . . pale," Jenny said.

Matt nodded, sat back on the ground to wait.

"I know. I'm sorry we couldn't stop this from happening, but we've called for an ambulance right away. And I ordered a car to take us home. I'm sure the detective will be too busy to come back for us."

Jenny dropped to her knees next to Sophie,

staring down at her, crossing her arms over her chest and grabbing her shoulders as if she were protecting herself. Even in the dark, Matt could see that she was trembling.

"Jenny. Are you all right?"

"She's so . . . pale," she said. This time when she said it, Matt could hardly hear her.

D etective Flynn pushed by Matt as soon as he opened his front door.

"Where is she? How is she?"

"I'm here. I'm fine, Bobby, really."

Jenny looked up from where she sat in Matt's recliner under a blanket, a pillow under her head, and took Flynn's hand when he knelt on the floor beside her.

"What happened to you?"

She swallowed, shook her head. "Nothing. I just feel a little panicky inside. Nothing . . . to worry about." She forced a weak smile. "Did you catch the bad guys? How is . . . Sophie? Her face was so . . . pale."

"I caught 'em, and Sophie will be okay. The doctor said it was good that we called for help as quickly as we did." Flynn smiled at her, then snapped his head up toward Matt. "Jenny's having some kind of a panic attack, Matt. Why did you bring her here and not the hospital?"

Matt lifted his hands. "She refused, and my place is closer. Hey, you left my door open."

Matt returned to the entryway.

He meant to close the door. He had his

hand on the doorknob. But someone was standing there. A young woman with short, blonde, curly hair and dark gray eyes flecked with gold, her face bathed in the soft glow from his porch light, was standing on his stoop looking up at him.

"Who . . .?"

He swallowed the question, his breath catching, his mind screaming the answer at him. He didn't need to ask. He only needed to look into this woman's eyes. Except, he didn't need to search *behind* the eyes this time. He didn't need to search at all.

"Hello, Matt," she said. "Can I come in? That woman sounds like she may need my help."

Elliott Barnes had been warned by the Sunnyside staff several times about leaving his cigarette burning in a rec room ashtray, but whenever he got caught up in a fierce game of Hearts he often forgot. When the fire department determined that the likely cause of the rec room fire had been a smoldering cigarette, Elliott felt responsible, becoming increasingly despondent to the point that now when he needed surgery, he refused treatment, telling his daughter that he shouldn't be allowed to continue living. Exhausting all other avenues, Susan had reached out to the elusive T.E.S. Institute who claimed cases like Elliott's were their specialty.

Tess took a seat beside her client and took his hand in both of hers, giving him a gentle smile before closing her eyes and allowing her consciousness to flow into his. She always allowed the client's mind to take her where it wanted to go first to ease her way into their memories. Even though Elliott didn't consciously perceive her presence, his subconscious guided her to a time in the past where it wanted to dwell, to a happier time at Sunnyside when Elliott spent his days conversing with his friend Chester James and Chester's grandson Matt who often came to visit.

Tess knew she shouldn't linger in that happy time. She should ignore Elliott's subconscious and search for memories of the past that led up to the fire. But she became increasingly reluctant to do so. Like Elliott, she found herself wanting to remain a little longer, to keep listening to Chester's grandson read aloud from his journal, to continue enjoying his smile and hearing his laughter, to feel caught up in the joy and love exuding from him when he reminisced with his grandfather.

She had a crush on Matt James, to be sure. But she gave herself permission to indulge in its emotions, allowing them to overtake her, for she had the luxury of staring at him without reservation, hidden in Elliott's mind, her heart fluttering. Matt was unaware of her, and he would never know of it. When she finished her mission and returned to her present, his future, all she could take with her were her memories and her feelings for him, her private, precious secret.

Chester James passed away. Matt stopped visiting. Tess resumed her mission.

When she opened her eyes, she squeezed

Elliott's hand.

"It wasn't your fault, Mr. Barnes," she said. "The reason you couldn't remember rubbing your cigarette out in the rec room is because you finished your cigarette outside and tossed it in the ash can."

"I did?" He blinked, then turned to face his daughter and smiled. "I did do that. I remember that now."

Susan gave her father a long, tight embrace, then came around the bed to grip Tess's hands. "Thank you, so much. I've already sent payment to the Institute."

"No need to thank me. I'm happy to help."

Susan opened the drawer of the nightstand and grabbed an envelope, pressed it into Tess's hands.

"You said you paid," Tess said.

Susan shook her head. "It isn't payment. This is a letter I've been asked to give to you once you helped my Dad and not before. I didn't read beyond my instructions. But I have a feeling it might be important for you to read it now, before the Institute sends a car for you."

Tess withdrew the pages and unfolded them, her eyes widening. Was she seeing her own handwriting?

She read it, aware that both Susan and Elliott watched her, and when she reached the last page and scanned the seven unfamiliar names listed there, she turned the envelope over and read the address the letter had told her would be there.

She turned her mouth up in a small smile. Of all people, she shouldn't be surprised to be reading a letter written by her future self with advice for her current self, yet she marveled at the odd sensation it gave her.

"I hope it isn't bad news," Susan said. "I hope I followed the instructions correctly by asking Matt to write down his address."

"You did the right thing," Tess said. She smiled again, a little wider this time. "It isn't bad news at all. Just . . . unexpected."

These are the seven people you'll help if you stay with the Institute. I've listed them because you can still help them. You don't need the Institute to do that. But this moment might be our one chance to be with Matt, future Tess had written. *I hope you don't pass it up.*

Tess looked over at Susan who stared at her with wide eyes, and hesitated.

Read it now, before the Institute sends a car for you,

Susan had said.

Yes. If she were to act, the time was now.

She refolded the letter and replaced it in its envelope before crushing it to her chest.

"Susan, can I ask you take me to this address?"

Now, after waiting for hours on a bench down the street from Matt's house, waving bus after bus on its way and watching as the sun was replaced by the moon and stars, she stood in front of him at last, gazing up into the face she had just secreted away as a precious memory mere hours before, rewritten timelines course correcting to bring her to this moment.

Matt stuck his fingers into his hair.

"Is it really you?"

She didn't often cry or tear up. She had witnessed so many people's sad, traumatizing events that she had learned to distance herself. But no rules seemed to apply when it concerned Matt James. The tears came and stung her eyes and she blinked one batch away only to have another replace it.

Then she laughed, another act she found little reason to do often, at least around other people, and she was around so few people as just herself.

"Yes, it's me. That letter you gave Elliott's daughter was a letter I wrote to myself. I told myself to come here."

She shrugged, holding her shoulders aloft waiting for Matt to speak, to tell her if he even knew what she was talking about, watching him as he stared down at her, slack-jawed.

"Matt. Is someone at the door?"

Tess recognized the voice as belonging to the man she had just seen burst into Matt's house, the one she heard telling Matt that he should have taken someone named Jenny to the hospital.

Tess let her shoulders drop and drew in a breath.

"If you let me in, Matt, I think I can help."

"Oh." His eyes went wide. "Oh, man. I've just been standing here like an idiot. Come in. Come in."

She stepped into the entryway and Matt closed the door behind her, gestured toward the living room before running his hands over his hair, either attempting to smooth it into place or for something to do to keep his hands occupied.

He moved up beside her. "Jenny." He

waited until the woman in the recliner turned her attention away from the man kneeling at her side. "Jenny, this is *her. Not Jenny.*"

Tears pinpricked her eyes again at the sound of Matt's excited voice, even as she wondered what he meant by "Not Jenny."

The woman focused on her, her mouth moving as if she wanted to say something in response but couldn't find any words.

Tess knelt on the floor, taking a position on the opposite side of where the man sat, and took Jenny's hands in hers. Jenny didn't resist, but the man reached out and grabbed Tess's arm to pull her hands away.

"What are you doing? Who are you?"

Matt gripped his shoulder.

"It's all right, Detective. She can help." Matt pointed to the couch. "Let's sit over here, why don't we, where we won't disturb them?"

The detective switched his gaze from Tess to Matt and back again, then released her arm and stood. "All right, for now."

When the two men had taken their seats on the couch, Tess turned back to Jenny.

"Hello, Jenny. You can call me Tess. If you would close your eyes for me? I know it's hard to relax the way you're feeling, but just breathe and listen to your heartbeat and imagine it beating slower with each breath. That's all you need to do."

When Jenny closed her eyes, Tess closed hers.

The memories she needed to target gleamed like a beacon. Tess hadn't expected the path to be so clear, especially in one who still retained relatively coherent thoughts, but the memories beckoned to her as if they had been waiting a long, torturous time to be discovered.

As soon as her consciousness flowed into the glowing memories, she saw what Jenny had seen and knew what Jenny had thought as a young girl lying on the floor of her bedroom, lost in a work of art of crayon and marker and stickers, glue, and glitter. The birthday card she was creating would be beautiful. Her mother would smile and praise her. Her little brother would only draw a simple scribble on his card and his Mother would smile and pat his head, but she wouldn't love his card the way she would love Jenny's.

"Your brother's getting in the shower now, Jenny. Listen for him and when he's finished, help him dry off."

"Yes, Mother."

Jenny nodded but didn't look up. She heard her mother turn the shower on in their shared bathroom, then heard her close the door as she left. She heard her brother's elongated yawn, but then could barely hear him after that over the sound of the water.

More purple in the rainbow, a yellow sun, a house with glitter on the roof, and inside a three-tiered cake with candles with sequins to represent the flames.

"Jenny, where's your brother?" Her mother had returned.

"In the shower," Jenny said. As she said it, she realized how much time must have passed. "But the water's still . . . running."

"Still?!"

Jenny dropped her card and ran to the bathroom just a step ahead of her mother. She shoved the shower curtain aside and found her brother lying sprawled on the tile, cold water raining down on his deathly pale face. She reached out and touched his shoulder. He felt as cold as ice.

Her mother pushed her aside and shouted her brother's name, a second and third time, grabbing him up into her arms, yanking a towel from the rack and throwing it around him.

"Mom?" Her brother's eyes opened.

"What happened? Did you fall? Did you hit your head?"

Jenny's mother was crying, frantically searching through his hair for any sign of a wound, but there was nothing.

"I was tired," he said. "I fell asleep."

Jenny dropped onto the cold tile of the bathroom floor and leaned against the wall, tears streaming down her cheeks with no sign of stopping.

He looked dead. He was so pale. He had looked dead.

A long time passed it seemed before her mother returned and sat on the floor next to her and patted her hand, sighing.

"Well, that was scary, wasn't it? But it's all right, Jenny. He's fine. Silly boy, scaring us like that." Her mother curled her arm around her shoulders. "Everything's fine now."

Tess withdrew, satisfied that the memory had retreated gently to the place where it belonged, and meant to return to the present, but another memory blinked at her from behind a veil of thoughts. She sought it out, touched it – if one could describe thoughts as being tangible – and it felt eerily familiar. It was Jenny's memory, it had to be, and yet it wasn't. It was more of a latent imprint of someone else's memory. And it wasn't the only one.

Tess opened her eyes, squeezing Jenny's hand as a signal that she too could open her eyes, then released her.

The detective must have only stayed on the couch a short time, for he was kneeling on the floor by Jenny's side again, his expression pained in anticipation.

Jenny opened her eyes and focused on Tess, putting a hand over her mouth, then placing it on her flushed cheek.

"Oh my god. I had forgotten about that time with my brother and the shower," she said.

"Your conscious mind didn't want to remember, but something must have triggered the feelings from that memory just the same," Tess said. "You panicked because you didn't know where those feelings were coming from."

"Sophie looked so pale, and the water was splashing on her face. She looked just like my brother looked when I thought . . . " Jenny shook her head, unwilling to say the words, then her eyes grew wide. She sat upright and grabbed Tess's arm. "I remember other things now, too, except nothing related to my brother. I remember being here in this very room, like in my dream that wasn't a dream, except I remember talking to Matt about his journal, and talking about 'Jenny' as if I was talking about myself in third person. I remember looking at Matt and feeling so sad, like I was going to lose him."

"What did you say?"

Matt sprang to his feet and came toward them, bashing his leg into the coffee table with a thud.

"I saw those same memories," Tess said.

She hadn't intended to mention it, in case she had misinterpreted those imprints, but now that Tess had uncovered them, Jenny could remember being possessed while Tess recognized herself as the one who had possessed her. Except, it had been a future self that no longer existed now. Just as the future self who had written the letter no longer existed.

Matt took a step closer to her and reached out, perhaps intending to take her hands or touch her shoulders or even pull her into his arms, for his expression looked desperate to do one of those things, then clenched his empty fists at his sides instead.

"You saw memories of when you were *Not Jenny*?"

"*Not Jenny.*" She smiled. "Ah. I get it now."

She pushed herself up off the floor and stood in front of him, still needing to lift her head to look up at him. She stared, unabashedly, as if she were still hidden from view behind someone else's eyes. And Matt stared back, the silence between them fraught with simultaneous disbelief and joy that they stood face to face. This moment was both their first meeting and their reunion.

"I don't know if I should shake your hand, or hug you," Matt said.

His voice had been a deep-throated whisper.

"Take me home, Bobby," Jenny said. She extricated herself from the recliner, the detective helping her to her feet. "My place or yours. It doesn't matter. I have it on good authority that we'll be sharing a place soon anyway."

The detective lifted his eyebrows. "We will?"

"At least, I'm hoping that timeline still plays out." Jenny placed a hand on his cheek and smiled at him, then led him and his confused face toward the entryway, patting Matt's upper arm and then Tess's when she passed them. "I'll let you two get reacquainted. I'm going to go call my brother, and my mom. I need to hear their voices. Matt, I'm trusting you to tell me everything."

Then Jenny beckoned Matt to lean forward and whispered in his ear, then left, the detective opening the front door for her then closing it behind them.

They were alone. It was just the two of them, standing in Matt's living room where it had all started, at least where it had started for Matt. The girl from the future whom he had referred to as *Not Jenny* stood in front of him at last, more beautiful than he had imagined in all his musings. He loved her curls, her expressive eyes, and more than anything the way she made him feel when she looked at him.

She swallowed, appearing nervous suddenly, clasping her hands together in front of her.

"You must think me presumptuous just to show up here. I could call my handlers at the Institute and they'll come get me. I'm not sure what my future Tess thought I should expect from you, but it probably doesn't seem fair –"

Matt stepped forward and pulled her into his arms.

I'm not a hugger, Matt, Jenny had whispered to him. *But you are, and you both look like you need one.*

Matt pulled *Not Jenny* – no, Tess – even closer, and she relaxed her shoulders and leaned against him, releasing a small sigh of both relief and contentment.

"I don't know which memories you saw, if you saw anything about my journal, but I wrote to you for a long time after the timeline changed, when I thought you might read it someday. I've been waiting for you all this time, so don't go. Please stay."

He felt her head move against his chest in a nod.

"I want to stay," she said.

The fake grandfather's clock in his bedroom chimed. The day would soon be giving way to a new one.

She spoke again, her voice slightly muffled, and he drew his head closer to hers to hear her.

"Future Tess told me in the letter that I have seven people I need to help if I left the Institute. Will you help me do that? And I want to help more too if I can. I never really cared about the Institute, but I liked helping people, like Jenny."

"Of course. We can get the detective to help us, too."

"And one more thing, Matt, if you don't mind."

"Anything."

45

She pushed away from him just enough so she could look up at him, her eyes scanning his face with the look that felt so familiar. Except the look she gave him now was just the sweet without the bitter. Happy to see him. Only happy to see him.

"Can I read your journal?"

When You Were *Not Jenny* Again

ABOUT THE AUTHOR

Ann Bernath

 Inspired at an early age to write a book by an episode of The Patty Duke Show, Ann has been writing ever since. In 2023, two of her short stories were published in the TechLit anthology "Inner Space and Outer Thoughts: Speculative Fiction by Caltech and JPL Authors" inspiring her to share her work.

Ann lives with her husband in Southern California close to her two sons and four grandchildren. When she isn't writing, her hobbies include boardgames, painting miniatures, anime, and reading lots of manga.

Contact the author at readannbernath@gmail.com

OTHER WORKS BY THE AUTHOR

- "Inner Space and Outer Thoughts: Speculative Fiction by Caltech and JPL Authors"
  - "When You Were *Not Jenny*"
  - "Encounter: Return to Titan"
- "Rock. Stone. Pebble.," a Western adventure with a twist.
- "The Dragon King Invites You to Tea" – in progress as of this printing, published chapter by chapter on Kindle Vella.

Visit **readannbernath.com** for access to more stories and updates on works in progress, including a sci-fi prequel to "Rock. Stone. Pebble." titled "The Guide to Palas."

Made in the USA
Columbia, SC
25 October 2024

44678392R00059